P9-CRK-284

Father Gander

NURSERY RHYMES:

The Equal Rhymes Amendment

By Father Gander
Full Page Illustrations by Carolyn

Advocacy Press, Santa Barbara, California

JE398.8
F

For Elisa, Jason, John,
and all their little sisters and brothers
in our world

Copyright ©1985 by Dr. Douglas W. Larche
All rights reserved. No part of this book may be reproduced in
any form without permission in writing from Advocacy Press,
P.O. Box 236, Santa Barbara, California 93102, except by a
newspaper or magazine reviewer who wishes to quote brief
passages in a review.

 Published by Advocacy Press, P.O. Box 236,
Santa Barbara, California 93102
Advocacy Press is a division of the Girls Club of Santa
Barbara, an affiliate of Girls Clubs of America, Inc.

GIRLS CLUBS OF AMERICA, INC.

Book design, cover, calligraphy & auxiliary art by Janice Blair.

Printed in Hong Kong.
Library of Congress Card No. 85-727-85
ISBN 0-911655-12-3

TABLE OF CONTENTS

Foreword

Change Mother Goose? Who would dare? The wrath of generations of children and parents would descend upon you!

Yet the history of Mother Goose has been a history of change. No one knows with certainty whether there even was a person named 'Mother Goose'. The collection now bearing her name consists of bits of folk songs and remnants of custom and ritual. Some are rhymes written to commemorate an historical event or to comment on the politics or religion of the day, written for adults, not children. Only those consisting of rhyming alphabets, lullabies or games for children like "Pat-a-cake" were truly created for children. And what is more, literary versions of Mother Goose from before the 18th century differ substantially from each other in content because they were passed along orally.

Mother Goose as we know the collection now did not become a household word until the second half of the 19th century. As more and more people learned to read, the very readable collection of whimsical and often nonsensical rhymes grew in popularity. The child-like simplicity, melody and charm of the rhymes distracted readers and listeners from the frequent unsuitability and insensibility of the words for little children. The sing-song qualities and resulting enchantment lulled people into ignoring the occasional messages of violence, sexism and discrimination.

We have come a long way in battling discrimination and sexism, but the battle is not yet won. All of us have a responsibility to see to it that our children grow up unbiased toward another's age, color, sex or religious preference. We have a responsibility to reinforce the message to our children that their own talents and the development of them will decide their success in life, not their skin color or sex. Nursery rhymes can be a powerful socializing force in children. In the innocence of early childhood it is vital that nursery rhymes in their subtle but simple way implant the ideals we espouse. The words of "Peter, Peter, pumpkin eater" do not reflect the message we would give our sons about marriage, nor would we really want our daughters to think that only a Jack can jump over a candlestick. These are formative years for children. Let them hear noble messages.

Certainly the early versions of Mother Goose should be preserved in literary history for what they were, commentary on the times done fancifully in rhyme. For today's children it is time to take the delights of the old Mother Goose and apply them to the ideals we all want our children to have—equality, love, responsibility, an appreciation of life and all living things, good nutrition and conservation of resources.

Mother Goose has survived because of its musical and poetical merit, not its message. Why not take the best of the old and meld it with positive messages of work, love and ethics? Father Gander has done just that.

About The Author

"Father Gander" is Dr. Doug Larche, whom the *Waterloo Courier* called a "latter day renaissance man." He is an eclectic collage of poet, professor, playwright, songwriter, director, actor, coach and family man.

Dr. Doug holds a B.A. from Graceland College, an M.Ed. from Wichita State University, and a Ph.D. from Indiana University, his father's doctoral alma mater. A former Executive Director of Very Special Arts Iowa and Educational Consultant for the Iowa State Department of Public Instruction, Doug is currently professor and chair of the Speech and Theatre Department of Grand View College in Des Moines, Iowa.

His poem, "Tomorrow's Child of Joy" has received national publication and acclaim, and his "Louisiana Phoenix" was commissioned by the State of Louisiana Department of Education. Doug has written many songs and jingles, composed and performed on the record album, A NEW SONG, with his brothers, and uses music in all his workshops. He has also written several scholarly articles, booklets, plays, choral readings, readers theatres, teleplays, a screenplay, multi-media shows and journalistic essays.

A visually impaired artist, Dr. Doug is an erstwhile performer on stage, screen, radio and television, and has directed successfully in each medium as well. He has delivered hundreds of addresses and workshops on equity, arts, disabilities, human communication, energy and education all over North America. He is currently American Chairperson of the International Society of Energy Educators.

About The Illustrator

"Carolyn" is illustrator Carolyn Marie Blattel, and she is as unique as her fanciful drawings. Self-trained as an artist, Carolyn has a special purview as an achondroplastic dwarf. "Fantasy," she says, "is what I think the rest of the world looks like . . ."

With her technical pens, colored inks and colored pencils, she is drawing her way into national prominence. She has won many art shows, and sold thousands of prints. Her "Tiny Forest" was chosen recently by the National Committee★Arts for the Handicapped, an affiliate of the John F. Kennedy Center for the Performing Arts, for inclusion in a national exhibit originating in Rockefeller Plaza and then touring the United States. Carolyn has been selected as one of twenty artists nationwide to be featured in an exemplary publication of the National Endowment for the Arts/President's Commission on Employment of the Handicapped.

After much popular urging that her style was perfectly suited to illustrating children's books, Carolyn decided to embark upon FATHER GANDER NURSERY RHYMES. "A hidden Iowa treasure who won't stay hidden long," her work on this project was a labor of growth and love.

A sensitive, caring and private person, Carolyn resides with her son, John, who is also achondroplastic.

Introduction

"Jack be nimble, Jack be quick,
Jack jump over the candlestick!

Jill be nimble, jump it too,
If Jack can do it, so can you!"

"If Jack can do it, so can you," seems not to be an earthshaking philosophical dictum. Yet in a world where little girls are denied equal access to many of life's experiences — where they are forced behind veils, incinerated for lack of dowry, subjected to infanticide in outland China, this simple statement assumes greater significance.

The pursuit of equal rights is not just a popular American pastime. It is a pressing world issue of social justice and survival.

Nursery rhymes are among the first encounters with literature, cultural expectations and verbal stimuli that young children have. As such, they have an important and perhaps indelible impact upon the early formulation of perceptions of self, environment and relationships. Despite their fancy, innocence, and longevity, nursery rhymes offer a tawdry initial world view.

A study of one hundred of our most popular rhymes reveals a male-dominated, able-bodied, monocultural fairyland filled with sexism, anger, violence, environmental and nutritional ignorance and insensitivity to the human condition. The expectations are clear: girls may be flower-tenders, frightened curd-eaters, seamstresses, and imprisoned pumpkin shell residents, while boys can be kings, masters, candlestick-jumpers, scholars and wife-keepers. Boys dash off on adventures. Girls nurture children, staying pretty and unruffled. Girls can cry. Boys cannot.

It is time for a new paradigm. FATHER GANDER NURSERY RHYMES: the Equal Rhymes Amendment tries to do what the title implies — to amend nursery rhymes so they offer a more equitable world purview to children. Sometimes the amendment is as subtle as changing "he" to "they"; sometimes it is in offering answer verses to existing rhymes; sometimes it is in creating entirely new rhymes in response to current events. But always, this book attempts to preserve the whimsy, the innocence and the fun of Mother Goose. If Mother Goose can shake the dreamland tree, then so can Father Gander.

The fanciful illustrations of Carolyn Blattel include children from every race, ability and disability grouping, mainstreamed into a pluralistic faerie king/queendom which paints perceptions of equality for young minds.

This book tries to let little girls and little boys feel equally important. It attempts to provide shared experiences and expectations, create models of healthy relationships, encourage environmental and nutritional consciousness, suggest family planning, urge fair treatment of children and the elderly, teach acceptance of personal responsibility, illustrate the viability of the family unit, and demonstrate cultural plurality.

Can one small book of verse accomplish all these goals? Of course not. But perhaps when our children grow up, they will have more healthy perceptions than we have. Perhaps they will be freer to grant individuality and worth to all people than they otherwise might have been. Perhaps they will aspire to offer equality to a troubled world. Perhaps our mutual child may someday say, "If Jack can do it, so can I."

Father Gander

Jack & Jill Be Nimble

Jack be nimble, Jack be quick,
Jack jump over the candlestick!

Jill be nimble, jump it too,
If Jack can do it, so can you!

Sally & Bobby Shaftoe

Bobby Shaftoe's gone to sea, silver buckles on his knee.
He'll come back to be with me, pretty Bobby Shaftoe.

Bobby Shaftoe's fat and fair, combing down his auburn hair.
He's my friend forevermore, pretty Bobby Shaftoe.

Sally Shaftoe's gone away, to a job for equal pay.
She'll come back to me today, pretty Sally Shaftoe.

Sally Shaftoe's dark and thin, little dimples on her chin.
She's my friend forevermore, pretty Sally Shaftoe.

Curlylocks & Freckleface

Curly Locks! Curly Locks! Will you be mine?
You shall not wash dishes nor yet feed the swine,
But sit on a cushion and sew a fine seam,
And feed upon strawberries, sugar and cream.

Freckleface, Freckleface, I might be thine,
But help me wash dishes, I'll help feed the swine.
We'll sit down together at long workday's end,
And share our strawberries, for we are good friends.

Little Boy Blue & Little Girl Green

Little Boy Blue, come blow your horn.
The sheep's in the meadow, the cow's in the corn.
But where is the boy who looks after the sheep?
He's under the haystack, fast asleep.

Little Girl Green, come sound the alarm.
The fox in the nest and the chickens he'll harm.
But where is the girl who tends to the nest?
She's up in the hayloft, taking a rest.

Mary's Lamb & Bobby's Goat

Mary had a little lamb whose fleece was white as snow.
And everywhere that Mary went the lamb was sure to go.
It followed her to school one day, which was against the rule,
It made the children laugh and play to see a lamb at school!

Bobby had a baby goat whose legs were stout and strong,
And everywhere that Bobby went the goat would tag along.
It followed him to school the day that Mary's lamb was there,
The lamb upset an inkwell, the goat ate teacher's chair!

Banbury Cross

Ride a fast horse to Banbury Cross,
To see a fine lady upon a white horse.
Rings on her fingers and bells on her toes,
She shall have music wherever she goes.

To Banbury Cross, ride a fast horse again,
And you will meet up with a fine gentleman.
Rings on his fingers, his voice in the air,
He shall sing melodies sweet everywhere.

Cackle Goose, Cackle Gander

Cackle, cackle, Madame Goose,
Have you any feathers loose?
Yes I have, little fellow,
Half enough to fill a pillow.

Cackle, Mr. Gander, say,
Are your feathers loose today?
Yes they are, my lady friend,
Mine shall fill the other end.

Hickety Pickety

Hickety pickety, my black hen,
She lays eggs for women and men.
Sometimes nine, sometimes ten,
Hickety pickety, my black hen.

Humpty Dumpty

Humpty Dumpty sat on a wall,
Humpty Dumpty had a great fall.
All of the horses, the women and men
Put Humpty Dumpty together again!

Sleep, Baby, Sleep

Sleep, baby, sleep, thy father guards the sheep.
Thy mother shakes the dreamland tree, and from it fall sweet dreams for thee.
Sleep, baby, sleep.

Smile, baby, smile, thy mother guards a while.
Thy father tends the dreamland tree, and shakes a new sweet dream for thee.
Smile, baby, smile.

Pat-A-Cake

Pat-a-cake, pat-a-cake, baker's man,
Bake me a cake as fast as you can.
Roll it up and roll it up and mark it with a B,
And throw it in the oven for baby and me!

Pat-a-cake, pat-a-cake, baker's girl,
Take the dough and give it a whirl.
Roll it up and roll it up as long as you must,
And throw it in the oven for all of us!

The Old Couple Who Lived in a Shoe

There was an old couple who lived in a shoe,
They had so many children they didn't know what to do.
So they gave them some broth and some good whole wheat bread,
And kissed them all sweetly and sent them to bed.
There's only one issue I don't understand.
If they didn't want so many why didn't they plan?

Little Maid, Little Lad

Little maid, pretty maid, where goest thou?
Down in the meadow to milk my cow.
Shall I go with thee?
No, not now. When I send for thee,
Then come thou.

Little lad, handsome lad, goest thou too?
I'm off to the pasture, my own work to do.
Shall I go with thee?
No, not now. When I send for thee,
Then come thou.

Bo Peep & Joe Peep

Little Bo Peep has lost her sheep
And doesn't know where to find them.
Leave them alone, and they'll come home,
Wagging their tails behind them.

Little Joe Peep has lost his sheep
And doesn't know where to find them.
Let them learn, and they"ll return,
Wagging their tails behind them.

Baa Baa Black Sheep

Baa Baa black sheep, have you any wool?
Yes ma'am, yes sir, three bags full.
One for the minstrel and one for the dame,
And one for the children who live down the lane.

Wee Willie &
Wee Wendy Winkie

Wee Willie Winkie runs through the town,
Upstairs and downstairs in his nightgown.
Rapping at the window, crying through the lock,
"Are the children in their beds,
For now it's eight o'clock?"

Wee Wendy Winkie stands on the stair,
Watching and guarding the townspeople there.
If she sees danger she'll ring the town bell,
When peaceful she shouts,
"Eight o'clock and all's well!"

Deedle Deedle
Dumpling

Deedle deedle dumpling, my son John,
Went to bed with his stockings on.
One shoe off, one shoe on,
Deedle deedle dumpling, my son John!

Deedle deedle dumpling, Elisa Dawn,
Went to bed with her stockings on.
One shoe off, one shoe on,
Deedle, deedle dumpling, Elisa Dawn!

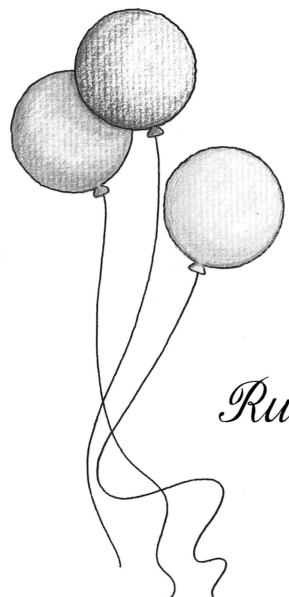

Run, Sister, Run

Run, Joanie, run,
Twenty-six miles.
When Joanie finishes,
All the world smiles.

Ride, Sally Ride,
Way up high.
Push our horizons
Beyond the sky.

Run, Geraldine,
The race begins.
Just by running,
Everyone wins.

Run, sister, run,
Run with your brother.
Not behind, not ahead,
But right beside each other.

Jack & Jill Finish the Job

Jack and Jill went up the hill
To fetch a pail of water.
Jack fell down and broke his crown,
And Jill came tumbling after.

Jill and Jack went up the track
To fetch the pail again.
They climbed with care, got safely there,
And finished the job they began.

Georgie & Margie

Georgie Porgie, pudding and pie,
Kissed the girls and made them sigh.
When the boys came out that day,
He asked them all to stay and play.

Margie Wargie, peaches and cream,
Hugged the boys and made them dream.
When the girls came out that day,
She asked them all to stay and play.

Little Ms. Lily

Little Ms. Lily, you're dreadfully silly,
To wear such a very long skirt.
If you take my advice you would hold it up nice,
And not let it trail in the dirt.

My dear helpful stranger, there's really no danger,
I'm wearing this skirt to a dance.
If I plan to be jumping and running and bumping,
I'll probably change into pants!

Peter Piper & Candace Carter

Peter Piper picked a peck of pickled peppers,
A peck of pickled peppers Peter Piper picked.
If Peter Piper picked a peck of pickled peppers,
Where's the peck of pickled peppers Peter Piper picked?

Candace Carter canned a case of candied carrots,
A case of candied carrots Candace Carter canned.
If Candace Carter canned a case of candied carrots,
Where's the case of candied carrots Candace Carter canned?

Mary & Larry Quite Contrary

Mary, Mary, quite contrary, how does your garden grow?
With silver bells and cockle shells and pretty maids all in a row.

Larry, Larry, quite contrary, how does your garden grow?
With white jonquils and daffodils and snapdragons all in a row.

Little Jack & Little Jane

Little Jack Pumpkin Face lived on a vine.
Little Jack Pumpkin Face thought it was fine.
First he was small and green, then big and yellow.
Little Jack Pumpkin Face is a fine fellow.

Little Jane Maple Face lived on a tree.
Little Jane Maple Face, happy and free.
First she was small and bare, then big and shady.
Little Jane Maple Face is a fine lady.

Blow, Wind, Blow

Blow wind blow, and go mill go,
That the millers may grind their corn,
That the bakers may take it,
And into bread make it,
And send us some hot in the morn.

Hot Cross Buns!

Hot cross buns! Hot cross buns!
One a penny, two a penny,
Hot cross buns!

Give them to your daughters, give them to your sons!
One a penny, two a penny,
Hot cross buns!

A Tale of Two Millers

There was a jolly miller, lived on the river Dee.
He worked and sang from morn 'til night, no one as gay as he.
And the song that he would sing, forever used to be,
"I care for nobody, no not I, and nobody cares for me."

He met another miller, from up the river Dee.
She worked and sang from morn 'til night, as happy as could be.
And the song that they will sing, forever now will be,
"I care for somebody, yes I do, and somebody cares for me!"

28

The Goodness Garden

Smiling girls and happy boys,
Come and try my little toys!
Celery Sally, Polly Pear,
Banana Binky, Collard Claire.
Connie Carrot, Mango Mick,
Gary Grape and Radish Rick.
Stephen Spinach, Brussels Bill,
Peggy Peach and Douglas Dill.
Nutty Nina, Penny Pea,
Cabbage Kym, Ben Broccoli.
Rhea Rhubarb, Bonnie Bean,
Pepper Pete, Tom Tangerine.
Chris Cucumber, Chestnut Chuck
And Hopping Jalapeño Huck.
Fiona Fig, Brandon Beet,
Princess Plum and Wendy Wheat.
Cheryl Cherry, Melon Mac,
Linda Lime, Zucchini Zach.
Oliver Onion, Turnip Tut,
And Happy Harry Hickory Nut.
Lisa Legume, Jujube Jon,
Yancy Yam, Tomato Tuan.
Heather Honey, Currant Caine,
Truffle Tess, Endive Elaine.
Jason Jasmine, Russet Raul,
Elisa Eggplant, Salad Saul.
Olive Okra, Rilee Rye,
Popeye Pumpkin, Veggie Vi.
Debbie Date and Parsnip Pam,
Barbara Berry, Scallion Sam.
Kendall Kiwi, Lentil Lan,
Witty Watermelon Juan.
Orville Orange, Prudence Prune,
Willie Walnut, Lemon Loon.
Duckwheat Duane and Juice Jenelle,
Dottie Deerfoot, Leek LaVell.
Black and Blue and Rasp and Goose,
Boysen, Elderberry Bruce.
Carolyn Corn, Ginseng Gene,
And Merry Myrtle Mustard Green.
Marie Mulberry, Peanut Paul,
And Erik Ernie Escarole.
Alice Avocado's Tot,
And Adam Aaron Apricot.
Michele McMushroom, Susie Squash,
And Smiling Scottie Succotash.
Pat Potato, Lettuce Lu,
And 'Rida Rutabaga too.
Asparagus Annie, Lima Lee,
And Arthur Artichoke for me.
Apple Andy, last not least,
Now what a tasty garden feast!

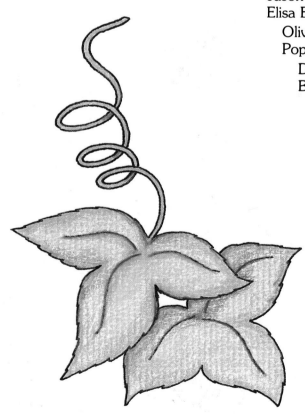

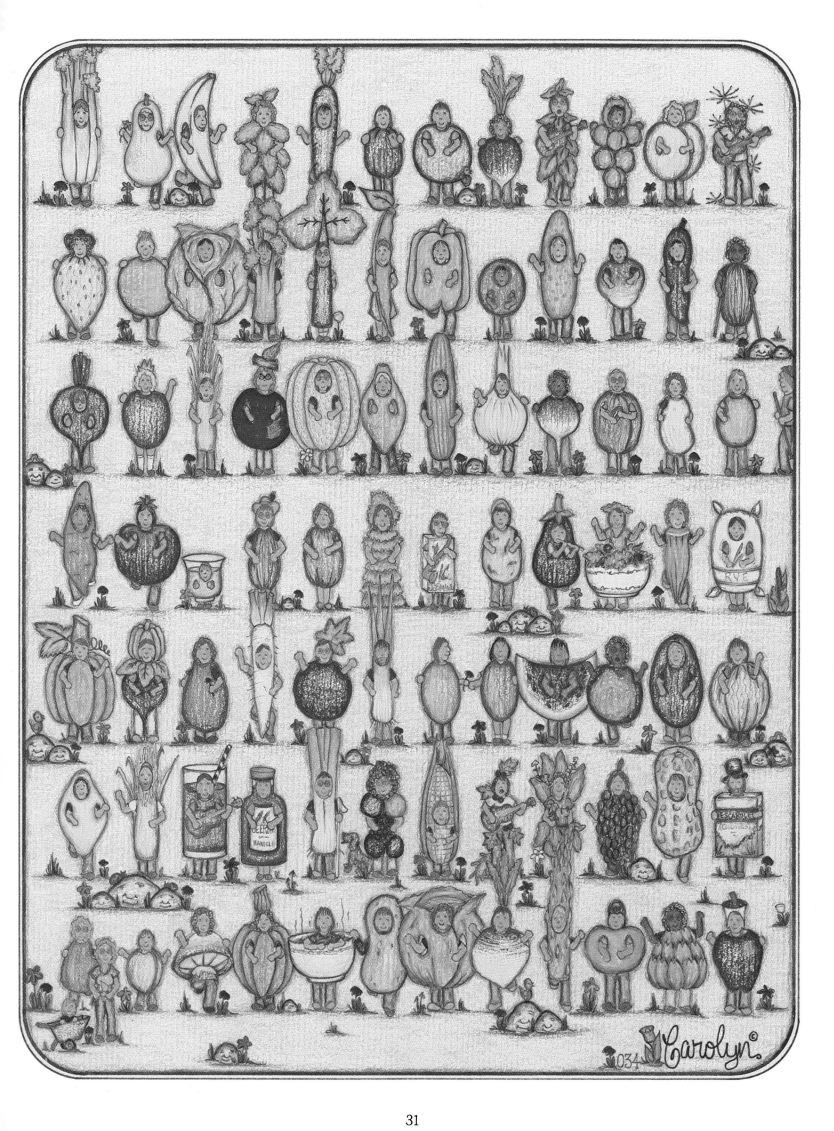

31

On A Saturday Afternoon

Sally go round the sun,
Sally go round the moon,
Sally go round the chimney pots
On a Saturday afternoon.

Jason go round the moon,
Jason go round the sun,
Jason go round the chimney pots
'Til the long afternoon is done.

Mandy's Mom

Mandy's Mom stays home to work,
Millie's Mom goes outside.
David's Dad is on the road,
Donald's Dad works inside.

A working Mother's really great,
A working Father, too.
A stay-at-home Mom is first rate,
Or a Dad who stays home with you.

Jumping Joan & Billy Bend

Here am I, Little Jumping Joan.
When nobody's with me, I'm always alone.

Here am I, Little Billy Bend.
When somebody's with me, I've got a new friend.

The Old Woman & The Old Man

There was an old woman, lived under a hill,
And if she's not gone, she lives there still.

There was an old man, lived high in a tree,
If he hasn't come down, he's still there to see.

Not the best way for the elderly, is it?
Their children and grandkids should come for a visit!

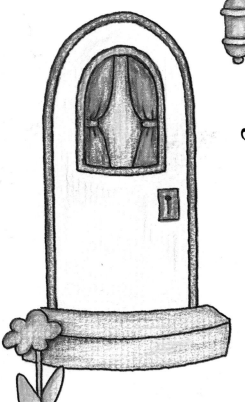

The Woman & Man Who Lived by the Sea

There was an old woman who lived by the sea,
And she was as merry as merry could be.
She did nothing but carol from morning 'til night,
And sometimes she caroled by candlelight.
She caroled in time and she caroled in tune,
And no one could hear her but the face in the moon.

There was an old man who lived by the sea,
And he was as happy as happy could be.
He did nothing but yodel from morning 'til night,
And sometimes he yodeled by candlelight.
He yodeled in time and he yodeled in tune,
And no one could hear him but the face in the moon.

35

Old Mother & Father Hubbard

Old Mother Hubbard went to the cupboard
To get her poor doggie a bone.
But when she got there, the cupboard was bare,
And so the poor dog had none.

Old Father Hubbard looked under the cupboard
To find the poor dog some relief.
But squint as he might, there was nothing in sight,
Alas, there was no bone beneath.

Mr. & Ms. Pumpkin Eater

Peter, Peter, pumpkin eater,
Had a wife and wished to keep her.
Treated her with fair respect,
She stayed with him and hugged his neck!

Tommy Snooks & Bessie Brooks

As Tommy Snooks and Bessie Brooks
Were walking out on Sunday,
Said Bessie Brooks to Tommy Snooks,
"Tomorrow will be Monday!"

The Piper's Children

The piper's children, Tom and Faye,
When both were young, they learned to play.
But the only tune that they could play
Was "Over the hills and far away.
Over the hills and a great way off,
The wind will blow our topknots off."
If they would practice some each day,
Then many songs they both could play.

Rub A Dub Dub

Rub-a-dub-dub, three folks in a tub,
And who do you think they be?
The butcher, the baker, the candlestick maker,
They've all gone off on a spree!

What Can the Matter Be?

Oh dear, what can the matter be?
Dear, dear, what can the matter be?
Oh dear, what can the matter be?
Johnny's so long at the fair.

He promised to buy me a bunch of blue ribbons,
He promised to buy me a bunch of blue ribbons,
He promised to buy me a bunch of blue ribbons,
To tie up my bonny brown hair.

Oh dear, what can the matter be?
Dear, dear, what can the matter be?
Oh dear, what can the matter be?
Jenny's too long at the fair.

She promised to buy me a cap of blue velvet,
She promised to buy me a cap of blue velvet,
She promised to buy me a cap of blue velvet,
To wear on my curly black hair.

Round About

Round about, round about, hot apple pie,
My father loves apples and so do I.

Round about, round about, cherry pie too,
My mother loves cherries, how about you?

Daffy & Dizzy

Daffy-Down-Dilly has come up to town,
In a yellow petticoat and a green gown.

Dizzy-Down-Dilly has come to town too,
In knickers and breeches of purple and blue.

Twinkle Twinkle Little Star

Twinkle twinkle little star,
How I wonder what you are.
Up above the world so high,
Like a diamond in the sky.

If the sky stays pure and clean,
We will see your twinkle bright.
But smoke, exhaust, and acid rain
All will cloud your flickering light.

Twinkle twinkle little star,
I'd like to keep you as you are.

I'm Glad to Help

I'm glad the sky is painted blue,
And earth is painted green,
With such a lot of nice fresh air
All sandwiched in between.

To keep the sky and earth and air,
One rule is absolute:
Conserve, protect, and use with care,
Try never to pollute.

Ms. Muffet & Friend

Little Ms. Muffet sat on a tuffet,
Eating her curds and whey.
Along came a spider and sat down beside her,
And she put it in the garden to catch insects.

43

If I Were an Apple

If I were an apple and lived on a tree,
I think I'd drop down on a nice child like me.
I wouldn't stay there giving no one my wealth,
I'd fall down at once and say, "Eat me for health!"

The Spratt Family

Jack Spratt could eat no fat,
His wife could eat no lean.
And so between the two of them,
They licked the platter clean.

Both Spratts, I'm sure of that,
Much better off would be,
To leave the fat upon the plate,
And be cholesterol-free.

Nell & Jack Horner

Little Jack Horner sat in a corner,
Eating his Christmas pie.
He stuck in his thumb and pulled out a plum,
And said, "What a good boy am I!"

Little Nell Horner sat in a corner,
Eating her tarts and jam.
She took a small bite and smiled with delight,
And said, "What a good girl I am!"

And though it is sweet, an occasional treat
Won't make your parents say, "Whoops!"
If you try every day to choose foods the right way
From the basic nutritional groups.

45

The Family Geese

Old Mother Goose, when she wanted to wander,
Would fly through the air with a very fine gander.

Old Father Gander, you soon will deduce,
Loved that fine woman, that Old Mother Goose.

The pair would discuss on their long flights around,
All the friends that they had, all the joys they had found.

They both had their dreams and their hopes and their needs,
And each let the other pursue them indeed.

They thus found fulfillment apart and together,
For at home or away they were birds of a feather.

They were each for each other; equals, the same;
He kept his "Gander", she kept her last name.

They planned a nice family, and loved it with care,
They both gave it nurture, the parenting shared.

They gave equal chances for adventure and joy,
To their little goose daughter and their little goose boy.

And all of the family shared this same notion,
That each should communicate healthy emotion.

When they made a commitment, they stuck to their word,
And yet when they finished, no bragging was heard.

Took care of the earth and their books on the shelves,
Took care of the air and took care of themselves.

They treated their neighbors as sisters and brothers,
They cared for their family and all of the others.

Respecting all cultures, all women and men,
They offered good will to their precious new friends.

They hope you will join them, and try to be good.
That's why they wrote this book, the best that they could.

And now that you've finished this quaint little piece,
You're sure to know better the "Family Geese."

46

A PERSONAL EPILOGUE

In 1972, Jason came into my life and set it on fire. Two years later, Elisa appeared and the fire exploded with unique new flame. A lifetime of chauvinism and male dominion came crashing into focus; even the nursery rhymes I read to my children would never the be same.

As my own consciousness began to expand, I had the joy of watching my father grow likewise, consumed by service to the disabled. My mother's life taught me selfless love and why women needed options.

To those of you who originally tried to help Father Gander fly, I offer thanks from the bottom of my heart. New family and friends began believing; the old never stopped. Somehow, we found the courage to try again. Then came Carolyn, who brought my simple words to magical, exhilarating life.

Treasured students, professors, colleagues, energy buddies, family and friends — my love for you fills up this little garden. Thank heavens for children, music, language and Eyes of Blue. Let us get on with the work of healing our world, loving each other and offering equality to all.

D.W.L. 1986

Books by Advocacy Press

Choices: A Teen Woman's Journal for Self-awareness and Personal Planning, by Mindy Bingham, Judy Edmondson and Sandy Stryker. Softcover, 240 pages. ISBN 0-911655-22-0. $18.95.

Challenges: A Young Man's Journal for Self-awareness and Personal Planning, by Bingham, Edmondson and Stryker. Softcover, 240 pages. ISBN 0-911655-24-7. $18.95.

More Choices, A Strategic Planning Guide for Mixing Career and Family, written by Mindy Bingham and Sandy Stryker. Softcover, 240 pages. ISBN 0-911655-28-X. $15.95.

Changes: A Woman's Journal for Self-awareness and Personal Planning, written by Mindy Bingham, Sandy Stryker and Judy Edmondson. Softcover, 240 pages. ISBN 0-911655-40-9. $18.95.

Mother-Daughter Choices: A Handbook for the Coordinator, written by Mindy Bingham, Lari Quinn and William Sheehan. Softcover, 144 pages. ISBN 0-911655-44-1. $10.95.

Women Helping Girls with Choices, written by Mindy Bingham and Sandy Stryker. Softcover, 192 pages. ISBN 0-911655-00-X. $9.95.

Minou, by Mindy Bingham, illustrated by Itoko Maeno. Hardcover with dust jacket, 64 pages with full-color illustrations throughout. ISBN 0-911655-36-0. $14.95.

My Way Sally, written by Mindy Bingham and Penelope Paine, illustrated by Itoko Maeno. Hardcover with dust jacket, 48 pages with full-color illustrations throughout. ISBN 0-911655-27-1. $14.95.

Father Gander Nursery Rhymes: The Equal Rhymes Amendment, written by Father Gander. Hardcover with dust jacket, full-color illustrations throughout, 48 pages. ISBN 0-911655-12-3. $15.95

Tonia the Tree, written by Sandy Stryker, illustrated by Itoko Maeno. Hardcover with dust jacket, 32 pages with full-color illustrations throughout. ISBN 0-911655-16-6. $13.95.

Kylie's Song, written by Patty Sheehan, illustrated by Itoko Maeno. Hardcover with dust jacket, 32 pages with full-color illustrations throughout. ISBN 0-911655-19-0. $16.95.

Berta Benz and the Motorwagen, by Mindy Bingham, illustrated by Itoko Maeno. Hardcover with dust jacket, 48 pages with full-color illustrations throughout. ISBN 0-911655-38-7. $14.95.

Time for Horatio, by Penelope Paine, illustrated by Itoko Maeno. Hardcover with dust jacket, 48 pages with full-color illustrations throughout. ISBN 0-911655-33-6. $14.95.

Mother Nature Nursery Rhymes, written by Mother Nature, illustrated by Itoko Maeno. Hardcover with dust jacket, 32 pages with full-color illustrations throughout. ISBN 0-911655-01-8. $14.95.

You can find these books at better bookstores. Or you may order them directly by sending a check for the amount shown above (California residents add appropriate sales tax), plus $4.00 each for shipping and handling, to Advocacy Press, P.O. Box 236, Dept. FG, Santa Barbara, California 93102. For your review we will be happy to send you more information on these publications. Proceeds from the sale of these books will benefit and contribute to the further development of programs for girls and young women.

JUN 1998

BOOKMOB. APR 2000

J398.8--F
Father Gander
    Father Gander nursery rhymes

Rockingham Public Library
540-434-4475
Harrisonburg, Virginia 22801

DISCARD
DISCARD

1. Books may be kept two weeks and may be
renewed twice for the same period, unless reserved.

2. A fine is charged for each day a book is not
returned according to the above rule. No book will
be issued to any person incurring such a fine until it
has been paid.

3. All injuries to books beyond reasonable wear
and all losses shall be made good to the satisfaction
of the Librarian.

4. Each borrower is held responsible for all books
charged on his card and for all fines accruing on the
same.